CHARLIE & MOUSE
LOST AND FOUND

By **LAUREL SNYDER**   Illustrated by **EMILY HUGHES**

chronicle books · san francisco

For Kittenhead Snyder Poma, Rest in Purrs —L.S.

Library of Congress Cataloging-in-Publication Data:
Names: Snyder, Laurel, author. | Hughes, Emily (Emily M.), illustrator. |
Snyder, Laurel. Charlie & Mouse (Series)
Title: Charlie & Mouse lost and found / by Laurel Snyder ; illustrated by Emily Hughes.
Other titles: Charlie and Mouse lost and found
Description: San Francisco : Chronicle Books, [2021] | Series: Charlie & Mouse | Audience: Ages 6-9. | Audience:
Grades 2-3. | Summary: Lost and found things are the theme of the day, from Mouse's missing blanket, to a large
friendly dog (which Kittenhead does not like), and finally a puppy (which Kittenhead prefers).
Identifiers: LCCN 2020041319 | ISBN 9781452183404 (hardcover)
Subjects: LCSH: Lost articles—Juvenile fiction. | Brothers—Juvenile fiction. | Dogs—Juvenile fiction. | Cats—Juvenile
fiction. | CYAC: Lost and found possessions—Fiction. | Brothers—Fiction. | Dogs—Fiction. | Cats—Fiction.
Classification: LCC PZ7.S6851764 Cm 2021 | DDC 813.6 [E]—dc23
LC record available at https://lccn.loc.gov/2020041319

Manufactured in China.

Typeset in Baskerville.
The illustrations in this book were rendered by hand in graphite and with Photoshop.

10 9 8 7 6 5 4 3 2 1

Chronicle books and gifts are available at special quantity discounts to corporations, professional associations,
literacy programs, and other organizations. For details and discount information, please contact our premiums
department at corporatesales@chroniclebooks.com or at 1-800-759-0190.

Chronicle Books LLC
680 Second Street
San Francisco, California 94107

Chronicle Books—we see things differently.
Become part of our community at www.chroniclekids.com.

Contents

SOMEWHERE

"Blanket is missing," said Mouse after lunch.

"Oh no," said Charlie. "Where did you leave him?"

"If I knew that," said Mouse, "he would not be missing."

"That is true," said Charlie.

Mouse was very sad.

"Don't be sad," said Charlie. "Blanket is *somewhere*. He can't be nowhere."

"That is true," said Mouse. "But how will we find him? There are a lot of somewheres."

"We will look in *all* the somewheres," said

Charlie. "We will look all day."

"Okay," said Mouse. "Thank you, Charlie."

"Happy to help," said Charlie. "Where should we start looking?"

"The house is a somewhere!" said Mouse.

"That is true," said Charlie. "We will look in the house."

Blanket was not in the house.

"The yard is a somewhere!" said Mouse.

"That is true," said Charlie.

"We will look in the yard."

Blanket was not in the yard.

"The playground is a somewhere!" said Mouse.

"That is true," said Charlie. "We will look in the playground."

Blanket was not in the playground.

Charlie and Mouse went home.

They sat on the front step.

"This is hopeless," said Mouse. "Blanket is nowhere."

"I am sorry, but I do not know how to get to nowhere," said Charlie.

Mouse was very, very sad.

Charlie put his arm around Mouse.

"Mouse!" said Charlie.

"Yes?" said Mouse.

"Blanket is right here," said Charlie.

"Blanket is on *you*! *You* are the somewhere that

Blanket was."

Mouse hugged Blanket.

"I did not know I was a somewhere," said Mouse.

"You're my favorite somewhere," said Charlie.

ERRANDS

It was errand day.

Charlie and Mouse were going places!

But not fun places.

They went to the post office.

There was nothing fun at the post office.

They went to the bank.

There was nothing fun at the bank.

Only some very small lollipops.

They went to the store.

There was nothing fun at the store. Until . . .

"Mouse!" shouted Charlie. "Look!"

Mouse looked.

"That," said Mouse, "is a dog."

The dog was big. The dog was brown. The dog

was all alone.

"I have always wanted a dog," said Charlie.

"Of course you have!" said Mouse.

"Everyone has always wanted a dog."

Charlie and Mouse looked at Mom, who was

looking at the dog.

"Can we keep him?" asked Charlie.

"Can we keep him?" asked Mouse.

"Please say yes!" begged Charlie. "He is lost and lonely!"

Mouse nodded. "He needs friends. And we are very good friends."

"We do not know that the dog is lost," said

Mom. "He might just be waiting for his people."

"He looks lost to me," said Charlie.

"He looks very lost to me," said Mouse.

"Let's wait and see what happens," said Mom.

Charlie waited.

Mouse waited.

They waited a long time.

Nothing happened.

"Well," said Mom. "Try to call him. See if the dog will come."

"Spike!" shouted Charlie. "Here, boy!"

The dog did not come.

"Jimbo!" shouted Charlie. "Dave! Barky! Boots!"

The dog did not come.

"Come ON!" shouted Charlie. "Snowball! Binky! Batman! Pete!"

The dog still did not come.

"Ohhhhh," cried Mouse. "Why won't you come, you big SILLY!"

"Nice work, Mouse!" said Charlie.

"Thanks," said Mouse. "I try."

"This was a very fun errand," said Charlie.

"That is true," said Mouse.

SILLY

Charlie and Mouse loved Silly.

Silly loved Charlie and Mouse.

Silly also loved Kittenhead.

Silly loved pouncing on Kittenhead.

Silly loved barking at Kittenhead.

Silly loved chasing Kittenhead up the curtains.

"Poor Kittenhead," said Mouse. "She looks scared."

"I don't think she likes it," said Charlie.

"No," said Mouse. "I don't think she likes it at all."

Dad came into the room.

"Boys, I think we should take Silly for a walk.

How about that?"

"I like that idea," said Charlie.

"But Kittenhead likes it even more!"

Charlie and Mouse walked Silly.

Then Silly walked Charlie and Mouse.

Silly walked Charlie and Mouse into a puddle.

Silly walked Charlie and Mouse into a bush.

Silly walked Charlie and Mouse into each other!

"Dad," said Charlie. "I think Silly has walked enough for today."

Dad nodded. "We can go home."

When Charlie and Mouse got home, there was a
boy on the porch.

He was a big boy.

"Millie!" the boy called, right away.

And Silly ran into his arms.

"Oh," said Charlie.

"Oh," said Mouse.

It was hard for Charlie to say goodbye.

It was hard for Mouse to say goodbye.

It was not so hard for

Kittenhead to say goodbye.

BOOP

"I miss Silly," said Charlie.

"I miss Silly, too," said Mouse. "It was nice,

having a dog."

"Yes," said Charlie. "I always wanted a dog."

"And then we found one," said Mouse. "But

only for a little while."

"Silly was a LOT of dog," said Dad. "And she already had a home. She did not need to be found for very long."

"I know," said Charlie. "But we are still sad she's gone."

"Maybe a cone will help," said Mom.

They walked down the street.

They walked past the puddle and the bush to

the ice cream store.

Charlie chose chocolate with rainbow sprinkles.

Mouse wanted the very same thing.

They felt a little better.

Then Charlie noticed something.

"Mom," said Charlie. "Dad?"

"What is it?" asked Mom.

"Silly was a LOT of dog," said Charlie. "But

what if we could have a LITTLE of dog?"

"Oh!" said Mouse. "That puppy is the

LITTLEST of dog."

"That is true," said Charlie. "And that dog is named Boop. You can just tell."

"Hi, Boop!" said Mouse.

"I do not know," said Mom. "Kittenhead might still be scared."

"Mom," said Charlie. "This dog is no match for Kittenhead."

"Kittenhead is tough," said Mouse. "She could sit on Boop. If she had to."

"Well, what do you think?" said Mom to Dad.

"Well, what do you think?" said Dad to Mom.

"Well, what do you think?" said Mom to Dad.

"Well, what do you think?" said Dad to Mom.

"It is a very good thing we found Boop," said Charlie.

"That is true," said Mouse.

"It is also a very good thing Boop found us," said Charlie.

"That is also true," said Mouse.

"You know what?" said Charlie. "I think we are the somewhere Boop wanted to be."

"Yes," said Mouse. "But Boop is also the somewhere WE wanted to be. And we did not even know it."

Charlie thought about that.

"I am not sure Boop knows she is a somewhere," said Charlie.

"We will teach her!" said Mouse. "We will teach her all about somewheres. And other things, too."

"Good idea," said Charlie. "But the first somewhere we should teach her about . . . is the somewhere to pee."

"That is true," said Mouse.